THE ONE & ONLY
WOLFGANG

FROM PET RESCUE TO ONE BIG HAPPY FAMILY

WRITTEN BY STEVE GREIG & MARY RAND HESS

ILLUSTRATED BY NADJA SARELL

ZONDERkidz

To Wolfgang, just look what you did.
—SG

To Robyn (a.k.a. Mom2), a champion for animals everywhere.
—MRH

To Aki, Minttu, & Pontus
—NS

ZONDERKIDZ

The One and Only Wolfgang
Copyright © 2019 by Steve Greig and
Mary Rand Hess
Illustrations © 2019 by Nadja Sarell

Requests for information
should be addressed to:

Zonderkidz, 3900 Sparks Dr. SE,
Grand Rapids, Michigan 49546

Library of Congress Cataloging-in-Publication Data
Names: Greig, Steve, author. | Hess, Mary Rand, author. | Sarell, Nadja,
   illustrator.
Title: The one and only Wolfgang / by Steve Greig and Mary Rand Hess ;
   illustrations, Nadja Sarell ; foreword by Jodi Picoult.
Description: Grand Rapids, Michigan : Zonderkidz, [2019] | Summary: The
   nine senior dogs, assorted chickens, rabbit, and pig making up Instagram
   sensation Steve Greig's menagerie find that, despite their differences,
   they belong together as one loving family. |
Identifiers: LCCN 2019000655 (print) | LCCN 2019001515 (ebook) | ISBN
   9780310768241 (ePub) | ISBN 9780310768234 (hardback)
Subjects: | CYAC: Pets--Fiction. | Toleration--Fiction. | Family--Fiction.
Classification: LCC PZ7.1.G7418 (ebook) | LCC PZ7.1.G7418 One 2019 (print) |
   DDC [E]--dc23LC record available at https://lccn.loc.gov/2018047888
LC record available at https://lccn.loc.gov/2019000655

Photos: Melissa Markle, M. Markle Photography
Art direction and design: Cindy Davis

Printed in China

19 20 21 22 23 24 25 /DSC/ 20 19 18 17 16 15 14 13 12 11 10 9 8 7 6 5 4 3 2 1

What if nine old dogs, a rabbit, a scruffy chicken,
and an old bossy pig lived as one big family?

MEET THE ONE AND ONLY WOLFGANG!

ENGLEBERT

Legs of a chicken. Heart of a lion.

LORETTA

Loves country music and cheese.

ENOCH

He's the size of a horse. He eats like a horse. He swears he's a dog.

EDNA

Fashion icon. Lives for movie nights and breakfast burritos. Her favorite color is glitter.

EEYORE

He might look sad, but he's the happiest Chihuahua in the world.

MELVIN

There's something EAR(ily) cute about him.

EDSEL

*Watches your every move.
Could be planning to take over the world.*

WAYLON

*Unaware. Loveable.
Always in the Way(lon).*

STUART THE RABBIT

*He's Stuart the rabbit.
He's not rabbit stew.*

DORIS

*Imagine your grandmother
as a poodle.*

BIKINI THE PIG

She's fabulous. Just ask her!

AND THEN THERE'S BETTY

*More of a movie enthusiast
than a real chicken.*

They were once unadoptable, but are now unstoppable. Together.
Each member of this family has a story. Long before they were found, adopted, and loved ... forever.

One by one they were brought in from the streets, shelters, and chicken swaps.
Now they share an old home in the city.

All of them grateful to be part of this big, quirky family.

And these old, wild ones take care of one another. They guard the house from pesky squirrels and the curious mail carrier.

And if there's mischief to get into, you know they'll find it. Bikini finds the flour in an open cabinet and tries her hooves at baking. Since every professional baker needs a helper, Edsel steps in.

Every member of the family gets in each other's way now and again. And Waylon does it best!
He trips every old dog in the house when he suddenly stops without warning.

Before you know it, there's an all-dog pileup. He doesn't do it on purpose, of course.
He's just a little unfocused. And no one holds it against him, because family forgives.

Sometimes they have to do things they don't want to do.
But family can get through anything when they work together.

And everyone in the family loves movie night. But no one more than Edna …

and yet she's the first to fall asleep.
Turns out the longest attention span belongs to a chicken. A chicken named Betty.

At night, these old, wild ones share the same bed and the same dreams.
Except Loretta, who always dreams of cheese.

And on Saturday mornings, Edna rallies the troops for her very favorite thing ...
breakfast burritos. Snow, rain, or shine, they pile into the old car.
Because burritos with your best friends is everything right with the world.

At all times and in all places, what means the most is that they're a team. It doesn't matter that Eeyore is eighteen years old, he feels like a puppy on the inside. Or that Doris is blind, because she can still see how much she is truly loved.

It makes no difference that Waylon can't hear, or that Stuart is a rabbit, or that Bikini is a pig, or that Betty is a chicken, because ...

Family
is
Acceptance

And it's perfectly fine that Melvin has no teeth, Edsel looks like a gremlin ...

and Edna has bad hair days six days a week.
Family loves you no matter what you look like in the morning!

Don't worry that Englebert is so small he could almost fit in a cup, and Enoch is so big all the others have to look up.

Families come in all shapes and sizes.

No matter how old, small or large, funny or different they look, they can all go for a stroll in the city as one big family, knowing that they belong. Because old is as cool as new when you have a family who loves you.

After all, family is everything.

A LETTER FROM JODI PICOULT

My kids joke that every time one of them left the house to go to college, we got a dog. That's partly true—I have three children and four dogs. Dudley, our oldest, is a Springer spaniel. Ollie, another Springer, was a gift from one of my publishers. Alvin was a rescue puppy destined for a kill shelter before he found his way to us. And our fourth dog, Harvey, we adopted while on vacation (Who goes on a tropical vacation and returns with a new dog?).

It was sometime after Harvey entered our lives that I fell deeply, madly, and truly in love with Englebert. My daughter followed @wolfgang2242 on Instagram and couldn't believe that I—dog lover extraordinaire—didn't. Well, I rectified that situation, and immediately became smitten with Englebert. To paraphrase Dwight Eisenhower, it's not the size of the dog in the fight; it's the size of the fight in the dog. Englebert was three pounds of pure fierceness, and I lost my heart.

I stalked Steve's Instagram account along with his other hundreds of thousands of followers and grew attached to the rest of his menagerie as well. Then one day, I wrote Steve a note, telling him that I thought his mission of rescuing senior dogs was incredibly inspiring. To my surprise, he responded: "If you're ever in the area, please let me know."

I had just been given an opportunity to meet Englebert in person! It took me maybe a week to find a speaking engagement that would coincidentally put me in his hometown … with a free morning.

Here's what I can tell you from my visit: Steve is just as amazing as he seems to be from his Instagram account. And although it's not easy to eclipse a heart that size, his furry and feathered family manages to do just that. From Bikini, to Waylon, to Melvin and Enoch—all of these animals have oversized personalities that attest to the comfort and safety they feel in Steve's care. But Englebert … well, it was love at first sight (at least for me), and I spent about three hours holding him in my palm, because that's how tiny he is.

Many people tout the benefits of adopting dogs rather than buying them from breeders. Steve goes one step further by reminding us that older dogs are just as rewarding as puppies. And I dare you to meet his senior dogs and not agree. Senior dogs may not have as much time to spend with their owners, but that just means that the love they give is concentrated. Stronger. Purer.

I hope that others will follow Steve's example, and when they go to adopt a dog, they'll make sure to meet not just the puppies, but the dogs who've lived a little … and could use a second chance at happiness. After all, as humans get older, our capacity to love only increases. Doesn't it make sense that this would be true of dogs too?

—**Jodi Picoult,** *New York Times* Bestselling Author
(and Godmother to Englebert)